Let's Go, Dear Dragon

Modern Curriculum Press
BEGINNING
TO
READ
Series

Let's Go,
Dear Dragon

Margaret Hillert

Illustrated by Carl Kock

Library of Congress Cataloging in Publication Data

Hillert, Margaret.
  Let's go, dear dragon.

  (MCP beginning-to-read books)
  Summary: A boy and his pet dragon celebrate the Fourth of July by going to the beach, having a picnic, and watching the fireworks.
  [1. Fourth of July — Fiction. 2. Dragons — Fiction. 3. Seashore — Fiction]
I. Kock, Carl. II. Title.
PZ7.H558Le   [E]   79-23672

ISBN 0-8136-5525-0 (Paperback)
ISBN 0-8136-5025-9 (Hardbound)

20 19 18 17 16 15 14 13 12   04 03 02 01

Get up. Get up.
This is a big day.
A big day for us.

Here.
Help me with this.
Make it go up.
Up, up, up.

6

And now come here.
Here is one for you.
You can have this one.

See what Mother and Father can do.
Mother and Father can make something.
Something good.
And we can help.

9

We work here too.
Father and I work.
The car looks good.

Get in the car now.
Get in with me.
We will ride, ride, ride.
We will have fun.

Away we go.
Away, away, away.
What a good day.

Here we are.
Get out. Get out.
We can play here.

Look what I can do to you.
No one can see you now.
No one can guess where you are.

See this.

I can make it go.

It can go up and up.

Get it. Get it.

16

Oh, my.
Look what you can do.
You are good at this.

17

18

We can do this, too.
Work, work, work.
We can do it.

Oh, oh, oh.
Help, help.
Look at us now.
You are too good.

Come with me now.
Come in here.
You will like it.

Go, go, go.
Help me go.
I like to do this.

This looks good.
I want this
        and this
            and this.

You are a big help.
A big, big help.
Now you have one, too.
It is good to eat.

Oh, look at that!
Do you see that?
Can you do that?
Yes, you can.
You can do it, too.

One, two, three.
GO!
No, that is not good.
That is too little.

Now, here we go.
One, two, three.
Oh, my! Oh, my!
Look at that!
That is good!

28

Here you are with me.
And here I am with you.
Oh, what a happy day, dear dragon.

Margaret Hillert, author of several books in the MCP Beginning-To-Read Series, is a writer, poet, and teacher.

Let's Go, Dear Dragon uses the 65 words listed below.

a	father	make	that
am	for	me	the
and	fun	mother	this
are		my	three
at	get		to
away	go	no	too
	good	not	two
big	guess	now	
			up
can	happy	oh	us
car	have	one	
come	help	out	want
	here		we
day		play	what
dear	I		where
do	in	ride	will
dragon	is		with
	it	see	work(s)
eat		something	
	like		yes
	little		you
	look		